Whispers of Time

Whispers of Time

Dr. Krishna Saksena

Ocean Books Pvt. Ltd.
ISO 9001:2015 Publishers

Published by
Ocean Books (P) Ltd.
4/19 Asaf Ali Road,
New Delhi-110 002 (INDIA)
e-mail: info@oceanbooks.in

ISBN 978-81-8430-566-1
WHISPERS OF TIME
by Dr. Krishna Saksena

Paperback edition
First, 2019

Price
₹ 150.00 (Rupees One Hundred Fifty only)

Printed at
R-Tech Offset Printers, Delhi

In the loving memory of my dear Brother,
Sri Gopal Hari Jauhari,
Who lived and worked for others only.

Editorial

"Walking through the generations that I have witnessed closely" is yet another gripping narrative by the author who is already known in the literary world. This book is the latest addition to a fascinating number of publications written by her over some years. Going through this tale is certainly a journey undertaken to discover unknown territories of human relationship with each other, with generations in conflicting passions to reach the ultimate goal.

The story unfolds itself. The style is crisp, the method dramatic and entertaining. We meet various characters on the threshold of changing generations. We get acquainted with them. The present generation live their life looking over their predecessors even as the "Old order changeth yielding place to new". Within the boundaries of time the life of each character is defined by the author in a persuasive and delightful way which makes the story of each individual very lively and thought provoking. The twists and turns in the plot are handled with ingenuity and deft dramatic touches. The nostalgia, the challenges, the deeply felt reminiscences, the questions, and the search- all these combine to enhance the perceptive value of this Book.

—Prof. Leena Roy,
Delhi University

Whispers of Time

It was a dreadful dismal night. Dark clouds were running from all directions to cover the sky and terrific sounds of lightning were breaking the hearts of all when Suchita started getting pains. Mr. Srivastava and the entire family became very nervous; the mother kept on telling her to take the pains down quietly and not to shout for she had produced seven children without a single shout. It was only in one difficult case the child would not come out despite taking severe pains. So, to take more pains down and that the child would come out safe, they dug a hole on the ground which used to be muddy and filled it with water. The mother sat over the hole so that more force could be put down. Then the child fell in the waters from where it was soon picked up. Such was Dadi's times. But nothing would console her as the pains became too severe for Suchita to bear. Her cries became louder and louder.

No rickshaw or tonga was available in such a nasty weather. So, Mr. Srivastava took his umbrella and started walking on the street. He took fast steps towards the doctor's house and on reaching the place, he rang up the door bell. The doctor wondered who it could be on the streets in such a bad weather. She went to open the door and was surprised to see Mr. Srivastava. He told her of his plight and requested her to help him. Those were the days when one always stood for the other. She immediately took out her umbrella and walked out. On reaching his place, she could hear the loud cries of Suchita from the stairs itself. It was a life without telephone, without mobile or without any such help of protection.

The doctor entered the house and was pained to hear the cries of Suchita. She washed her hands with soap and took out her shoes and entered the room where *dadi* was sitting helpless and in fear as to what would happen next. She started dictating the doctor. So, the doctor requested her to kindly leave the room. The doctor then strongly pressed Suchita's stomach. A severe pain brought from Suchita a loud shriek of pain, but together with it, there was the cry of a baby. A lovely small baby also came out giving immense relief to Suchita. In the joy of creation, Suchita forgot her labour pain that she was suffering from for the last few hours.

On the day of naming ceremony, *dadi* named her as Kiran which meant hope and light for the family. She was a girl and those were the days when girls were not much welcomed in the Indian family. But as she came after a long waiting of five years, all were very happy. The family had given up all hopes. They were all insisting upon Mr. Srivastava to marry again, but he was adamant that if he was destined to have children, he will get them from none other than Suchita.

Kiran came as a welcome surprise as she saved the honour of her mother. She grew up with lot of love and care from all sides. Baba taught her to fold her hands and say "Thank you God for all that you have given me." She also sang songs in the praise of God. She was gifted with a melodious voice. Those were the days when religion and traditions played an important part. Amma would see that she did not go wrong on any side.

Kiran loved her mother and often teased her. Whenever she wanted to wipe her hands and mouth, she would come, not using the towel hanging on the rope, but would run to use her Amma's *pallo*. When the mother would tell her that so many towels were hanging nearby, with a sweet naughty look, she would tell her, "You know Amma, the lovely smell that comes in your *pallo* is missing in the towels." Suchita would smile and give her a kiss. She was a darling of all.

Amma would easily wear her *sari* making pleats that she would tuck it inside. Then bringing the sari on the left shoulder, she would cover her head and again tucked it inside on the other side neatly. She would do it in no time. Sitting before the mirror, she would put a neat *bindi* on her forehead and some *sindoor* in her parted hair. This was all that completed her dressing up. She would always cover her head because *dadi* was there. It would become a *ghunghat* if Baba happened to come in. I asked Amma why she was doing all this. Amma would reply, "This is my respect for the elders."

Parents and sons and daughters-in–law were part of one whole. Parents were treated by the young with great respect. The sons considered them as their responsibility and took great care of the elders. Life was so simple, so real, so beautiful and so easy. Togetherness was the key note of the times. The young ones never called those living in the same vicinity as Mr. Srivastava or Dr. Gupta or Mr. Agarwal, but they were addressed as *Chachu*, *Mausa*, or *Bhaiya*. The ladies were addressed as *Ma*, *Mausi*, *Chachi* or *Tai*. Living nearby, they lived as close relations. No one hesitated if any help was needed. "Bhiku I will be late at night as it is my night duty. So, come over to my place, spread your bed next to your *chachi* as she gets scared of being alone." "No problem *chachu*. I will come with my younger brother." Problem of one was also the problem of the other. If anyone became sick, it was serious concern of the others also. They all worked and prayed for each other. Such was the beauty of life. Religious bent of mind, respect for the elders, love for the young ones, helping each other, and a smile for all were some of the basic features of this generation.

When Kiran was three years old, Suchita became pregnant again. There was great rejoicing in the family. Kiran had opened the way. To add to all this, the neighbours formed a friendly part, working for each other in times of difficulties as well of rejoicing. Traditions had to be followed very strictly. If I think of a generation before me, it was very strict and laughable. Life of the ladies had impositions that became a burden to them. A newly wedded cousin visited us. I told *dadi* to come and give her, her blessings. With great difficulty, she opened her tin box and took out her very precious Rupees twenty for the girl. She came and asked for the bride and was shown the one sitting next to Amma. She was surprised to see her for there was no *ghunghat* to cover her face. *Dadi* put back her precious money and returned. When Kiran asked *dadi* why she did not give her blessing she said "She was no bride as she had no *ghunghat*. The face was seen from a distance. There was no need to give her anything." It made Kiran to go into peals of laughter. But that was the trend of the day in *dadi's* time.

With every new generation new ideas with new traditions come up. After Kiran two daughters and two more sons were born. Prakash was the youngest and most pampered. *Dadi* and *Baba* would come to stay with us and every summer *papa* would make it a point to take us to *dadi*'s village. She had a huge house and Prakash, my younger brother and myself with other brothers and sisters, would run and break mangoes from the tree. We had a good time sitting on the cart, singing songs loudly and on reaching the *mela,* we bought small things. We had a great time in the village. *Dadi* would call Kiran and tell her that as she had grown up, so she should behave like a grown up girl and she should not be running about like a boy. She was made conscious that she was different from boys. She must change her behaviour. She must now stay with girls only. "My dear child I am like that tall *neem* tree standing here for a long period of time and silently looking at many incidents and events and speak from experience. She should not be running about like a boy. She then was friendly with the girls of the vicinity. They all stayed together and talked on various topics. Boys were not allowed to come near them. Often they were seen teasing and passing remarks, but the girls did not bother. The mother treated the sons differently and gave them special care. While at night, the boys were given *malai* the girls would get only milk. It was the system and the girls never felt bad. They were satisfied as that was the custom.

India was under the British rule and Kiran studied in an American missionary school where there was strict discipline. Kiran was seen to be weak in Geography which was reported to the father in reply of which, the father wrote back: "She is now under your care, it is you who needs to care for her." A teacher was appointed to bring her to the point. Such was the discipline of the school. All sat in their classes with full attention to what was being taught in the class. Can you ever imagine such a strict discipline in Indian schools now? The other sisters were also admitted in the same school. But the best in studies was Kiran. The boys were in a school that was only for the boys. There was no such thing as co-education.

Despite boys and girls being separated, there were love affairs which were not liked by the society and brought bad name to the parents.

They were all a contended lot and that was their bliss. Their happiness consisted in not possessing much, but being content in whatever little they possessed. He who had little had much. Rich and powerful had many secret problems. There was a powerful feeling for each other in the neighbourhood and at any time of difficulty, one stood for the other. Their happiness was to pray for each other.

There were strange rules of marriage. The boy was not allowed to see the girl whom he was supposed to get married to. It was only the mother who saw the girl and if she approved, the marriage was settled and her way of seeing was quite different. I remember my cousin who was very handsome getting married to a very ugly girl because the father gave a heavy dowry. For some time, he avoided his wife, but, finally, he had to come to her because the parents insisted.

My uncle became a milk-seller and came to my aunt's house, called out loud, "A milk-seller here, is milk needed? Do come up, fresh milk is here." And as the girl peeped out, whom he was to get married, he could see her and like a very obedient son, got married because he had seen the girl and approved of her. My brother had to become a beggar to see the girl he was to get married to. Such were the cases and many amusing incidents can be cited. Great was the role of the parents in every direction and in every situation. They were honoured and obeyed. Togetherness and life of service ruled their life and gave them happiness and a direction to move on.

It is the story of the times when we went to Mangal Bazar and had *chola bhatura* with hot *puries* only at the rate of Rupees 5 which was enough for the evening. Houses were small but hearts were large. Such words like space and privacy were words which people did not know the meaning of. All the upper house stories were joined together. We kept on walking in life showering smiles on each other. Even toilets were together. People knew the names of all the people living in the vicinity. One and a half dozen relations lived comfortably in three rooms. During holidays, others would also join. *Mong dal* with *ghee tarka*, all of us would eat to our full satisfaction after which they would drink cold milk, had a nice talk together and then they would spread their legs and go off to sleep on the beds, being laid down by their children. All would get up before sunrise, fold up their beds and go on their usual work. All of us had less money but immense happiness. We kept on walking in life showering happiness on all. We shared each other's happiness as well as their problems. We prayed for each other. Devanand was our popular hero and we sang songs that he sang, one would get a V.C.R. on hire, call all the neighbours and together we would see the film.

The main occupation of this generation was agriculture. To me, it appears that there are three ways to acquire wealth. The first is by war as it was seen in the case of Muslims and British people that conquered our nation which is nothing but robbery. The second is by commerce which amounts to cheating and the third by agriculture, the only honest way wherein a man receives a real increase of the seed thrown into the ground, in the kind of continual miracle brought in by the hand of God in favour of an innocent life and virtuous industry.

Marriage in any house would become a festival and a celebration for all. Wah what a scene, all sitting together, pealing peas, laughing, talking and merry-making! I remember my brother's marriage when all joined and as the bride entered the house, which ever instrument of music one had was brought in. Some had *tabla*, some had violin, some had harmonium, some brought in her flute and as *bhabhi* stood on the gate all broke together on a song: "Welcome dear *bhabhi* to your new home." It looked far more beautiful, far more meaningful than all the noisy meaningless orchestra of today.

Kiran passed out with a first division and distinction in maths. All were happy. Financial condition of the father did not allow her to join I.T. College, a continuation of her school because it was far away and the father could not afford a rickshaw for her. So, she was admitted in the Hindi medium college, namely Mahila College. Kiran was amazed to see the scene. With no discipline, all the girls had a gala time. First, Kiran was annoyed and told her father about it, but he was quiet for he had no other way and told her to pay attention to her studies. Kiran gradually started enjoying the freedom. The students attended the class if they wished.

One day her friend asked her to meet her brother. "Why?" She was surprised. "He likes you." "Me? My father will kill me if he comes to know about this." "He has passed out from a prestigious college and is looking for a good job. He has many offers but you know he is very selective." Surprised Kiran asked, "But my dear friend, why are you telling me all this. My father will kill me if he comes to know this." "Just meet him once," requested her friend. So, she agreed. Puneet came to meet Kiran, talked to him and they had an easy conversation. He insisted that she should meet often as they had so many topics to talk on. Kiran was drawn towards him knowing very well that it was against the tradition of the family, something that would hurt the reputation of the father. But, then, she argued within herself that there is no harm in meeting someone occasionally. Human heart conquers all traditions and one never realises that how it moves towards something what it never thought of.

They were critical days in the history of India. It was the time of Quit India movement. Leaders like Nehru, Patel and Subhash Chandra Bose were seen on the streets giving stirring speeches.

They were rousing men and women to see that they were slaves in their own country. Therefore, they must revolt and throw away those that have taken their rights. Now all, men and women, must rise and take away what rightly belongs to them. In Mahila College, where there was no discipline, girls rose up to march, left the classes to join the procession and took a very active part in this struggle. Hardly any class was held. It gave a good opportunity to Kiran to sit with his admirer Puneet to have long talks. They did not come so near as to hold hands, or kiss or to do any such mischief, but the expression of the eyes told each other that they needed one another which was not possible those days. Love marriages were looked down upon so badly that the father would be ready to commit suicide. But human nature could not be denied.

Partition spoiled all that was beautiful in India. While leaving India, the British people sowed seeds of hatred between Hindus and Muslims. Jinnah was denied the post of a prime minister, which led to partition. Gandhi agreed to Nehru, though he said in Noakhali that partition would be over his dead body. The division led to severe mass massacre.

Lakhs of people lost their lives in deportation. Their hands did not tremble as they planted the weapon of doom. Their hearts did not miss a beat when they witnessed the scenes of gloom. The man whom you had killed might have helped you as your brother. The violence and conflict that was witnessed were horrible. Muslims started the mass rampage, insulting the young Hindu ladies. Mr. Srivastava had three young daughters. So, they made an attempt to reach the ladies and insult them. The father closed the door and tried to fight with them. He was fighting a losing battle when Puneet seemed to pass that way. He came up and gave a tough fight to the invaders and saved the lives of the family of Mr. Srivastava. When things were safe, Srivastava invited Puneet to come in and have a cup of tea. Kiran brought the tea anxious to see who saved his father on that deadly day and was surprised to see it was none but Puneet. She never tried to show that she knew Puneet.

Simplicity is the key note of this generation. Beauty of style and harmony and grace, good rhythm depend on simplicity. No parlours are needed. Simple in looks, simple in dress, simple in their character and simple in their behaviour are the ways of life. Religion occupied an important place. Going to the religious places meant a true bent of the mind to learn and understand. The elders gave help to the young ones if they needed. Money is important but it never became the God that ruled the society. The hearts were soft for any that asked for help. Elders were respected. For the needy, for the women, help came from all directions. The youngsters were always ready to help the elders in all the homely jobs. Sadhus and seers led a life that set an example to others. They were heard and followed by the people. In spirituality, there was no deceit or bad intentions. They taught by the life they lead how to live a life that is meaningful. They gave advice on how to live for the good of others and for themselves, thinking high and leading a life that made them reach the heavens. Traditions had to be respected. Anyone moving away from these was looked down upon. But on the whole, life was easy and beautiful. According to Bhagvad Geeta, there are three gates to self destructive hell, namely lust, anger and greed, and this age was somehow away from such conditions.

Srivastava was an ordinary man with no money to offer huge dowry for a guy that was good and was from a rich and educated family. So if a good boy from a high family made an offer for his two younger daughters that were beautiful because of fair complexion. The parents readily accepted the offer without ever thinking of the feelings of the elder one. Not that Kiran was in any way ugly, but the sisters were more charming. Kiran had sharp features and was more attractive with slight fair complexion, but others had fairer complexion which was preferred much by the boys and the parents. Looking to their needs, they left Kiran and married two younger daughters regardless of the feelings of Kiran.

Kiran went for higher studies which she managed after crying and refusing to take food for a week. She was hurt badly and very deeply, but she concentrated on her work. Dirty comments were passed on her that made her very sad. Without giving heed, she was able to work hard on her thesis. The father was honoured as it came out in all the papers that she is the first woman candidate in the whole of U.P. to get that honour and she is the daughter of Prof. Srivastava. She was given a post in the Lucknow University. Many marriage proposals poured in from all directions, but Kiran's heart was with Puneet. But here the problem was with his caste. So, one evening when it was all around dark and was about to rain, Kiran eloped with Puneet. She did not look back as to what happened to the family and the reputation of the father. They had insulted Kiran and she did not care for them.

They ran to the extreme south. They performed a mandir marriage and lived happily. Both were highly qualified. So, they got good jobs. While Kiran got into the Madras University, Puneet worked as a high official in a government office. They had one son and one daughter and were happy.

An era seems to end when its basic illusions are exhausted and new thoughts and views came up and respected. An era of masculine dominance comes to an end and a feminine understanding of life's wholeness is included. It is a different world in which well being of all is included. The children were much doted upon and there was no difference between a girl and a boy. The boy was named Prabhat and the girl Jyoti. They were much attended and looked after. They grew up as conceited proud fellows. Jyoti at home was called *guriah*, taking up no responsibility of ever helping her mother even in laying up the dinner table. The mother never ever objected making her, self centred and conceited. The same was the story of Prabhat with the father. Both the children were put in best schools as the parents were earning well. The behaviour of the parents and children changed completely with the dawn of this new era as it entered giving way to the old. At times, Kiran would become very sad when she remembered her father on account of whom she got a degree that gave her position and honour. She wanted once to meet him and touch his feet and ask him to forgive her, but then, next moment she was scared and wiping her eyes of the tears that flew down, she went off to sleep. Puneet tried to console her, but it was a memory that lasted till her death.

With times now settled down after Independence, there was improvement to be seen all round. The standard of education improved. Jyoti took part in debates and discussions and got a number of prizes which made her still more confident and proud. But the true test of civilisation is not the census, nor the size of the cities, but the kind of people the country turns out.

Prabhat did not do well in his examination and got a very low position and was so much disappointed that he did not wish to continue his studies. Kiran wanted Prabhat not to get discouraged for she explained in so many ways that: "Our glory is in rising every time we fall. Many people who fail in life are those that did not realise how close they were to victory when they gave up. Equanimity means looking up at failure and success with the same eye. It is not what you do that defines you. What defines you is how well you rise after you have fallen."

To give an example is the life of your uncle. He wanted to become rich. So, in a business joined with a rogue who cheated him and his father so badly that they became penniless and were beaten mercilessly. Creditors started harassing the father who advised his son to run away. Penniless he ran off to a remote place where, to live, he took up the task of driving a wagon cart and ringing a bell to call people around and tell those that gathered, about an article that a small company was making. It was a shameful job for the son of a highly placed officer, but something had to be done to be alive. Taking unhygienic food, he lay in a small dirty hospital. He continued to work hard and got a place in a good company. Signing on some wrong document, he was sent to jail. Coming out of the jail, he got a better position in the company. With a good convincing power that would make the false as the only truth he kept on rising. He got a severe blow on the death of his father, when he left the place and job and came over to look after his mother and his mentally retarded brother. He got a good job in a big company. He became the head of the rising technology of the present times. Today, he has a lot of property, any number of cars and many servants to serve. He is in a position to have for his family a life of luxury and convenience. Today, he has defeated all that ran with him. He is the head of a technology that is both powerful and useful. His boss is fond of him for he finds him most competent in his work.

There are few like him that rose from dust to sky and have made a name. Dhirubhai Ambani, Modi to mention a few. You know, my child, anger deprives a sage of his wisdom and a prophet of his vision. But anger is a great force, if you control, it can be transmuted into a power that can move the whole world. So, my dear child, stand up and run and I am sure you can do wonders. "But *ma*, who are the men you are talking about?" "You do not know them. So, do not get into it, but they are as real as you are." In telling all this, my mother did not whisper into my heart. It was not my lips that she kissed, but my very soul.

Type of education had immensely improved after the turmoil of Hindu-Muslim riots had subsided. That brings you to things quite different. It brings you to easier days not of love and humanity, but of intelligence working hard in different directions. These were the days of technology bringing up new things, like phones, picture halls, CCTV cameras, aeroplanes, etc. These bring you to the days not of togetherness and a feeling for each other, but of pride and power working hard towards self-gain. The power within to tell that "I can do it" brought a change, something within goading them to go forward in their thinking and imagination which brought in marvels. You can achieve as much as you can, important thing is God's blessing. So, if you believe in God and in yourself, you have nothing to worry about. Do not put things for tomorrow, what you can do today. Time is equal to life, so do not waste it. Do master your time and, thereby, your life. You need to have central purpose in life. With this sort of feeling, Prabhat moved ahead and was successful in finding more functions that cellophanes were in a position to perform. He was a boy that preferred silence.

Learning received special attention and many good institutions came up with well-qualified teachers and a syllabus that easily made the youngsters knowledgeable. The students were selected to go to foreign countries for further studies. Life was following new values where there was an imitation of foreign characteristics. The old moral values were thrown to the winds and a new generation was coming up. The old was thrown out and youngsters ran after the new. 'Ring out the old and ring in the new', was the song of the day. The new society that was slowly emerging found that those values that were respected were tedious and hard and were not to be followed for the new values were easy and helpful. For example, the young need to look and care for themselves and the old were not their responsibility. In the company of the old, they felt frustrated and, therefore, the old must leave and also leave the young to enjoy life the way they wanted. The old and the new could not go together hand in hand. They broke by a heavy jerk and are never together. The youngsters lost their care and respect for the old.

Life was following new values and there was a lot of imitation of foreign characteristics. The old moral values that were good were thrown to the winds and a new society was coming up where we found that what we respected became outdated. The young need to care for themselves and they were no longer responsible for the parents. They need to look after themselves. They could not be happy in the company of the old people. So, old homes gradually became popular. The elders found no respect from the young who merely cared about themselves. The family of the five and seven disappeared and, instead, nuclear families came up. If you look at the moral values, there was definitely a deep fall. Togetherness gone, each cared for himself never ever concerned about the problems that concerned others and elders. Each has to care about his own problems. Standard of living was reducing as the impact of the movies was heavy, especially on the youngsters.

Dowry deaths were well known and quite popular. Huge money was demanded at the time of marriage from the girl's side to get a good boy. Sometimes the parents had to sell off their belongings in order to put the daughter at a comfortable place. At times, even after the marriage, they demanded more, failing which the bride was burnt and they told a cocked up story that it was just an accident. The greed for money grew to such an extent that murders were committed for its sake.

The most important word prevalent in this age is the word 'sex'. Sex was not known before and, if ever used it was with secrecy and shame. In manners and dress, the model was some actress in the movies. Teaching becomes more of a business than a way to guide people to move on the right path. In fact, it led the people to fool others.

The women of the past generation wore their dresses to cover their bodies in the best possible manner, but now all attempts were made to show off their bodies. Sleeves sent to the sky, shirts high up to make their bodies look prominent and pant so tight as to show and make the movements prominent. Sex is the key word all round. There is nothing wrong in sitting and enjoying with the boys and definitely adding a little pinch of wine for that would make the enjoyment double up.

Prabhat was looked down upon by his father for he was not good in his studies, but he loved his daughter as she was not only clever, but very good in her studies. So, if she needed anything, it was immediately given to her. She proudly sat in her room well equipped with the latest equipment. Her father asked her if she needed anything and often sat with her and talked to her. The mother often objected to this attitude, but he never listened to her. "My child, if you need anything, I would get for you because you are my darling." This would make Jyoti, his daughter, conceited and proud. The son Prabhat was considered useless and was called his mother's baby. Prabhat had views like his mother and was a boy of decent behaviour. He was often criticised by his sister who would say, "You better change your ways else no girl will even look at you." To which the brother would reply, "I do not care for that, but you need to change yourself, else getting Papa's pampering you may one day surely land in trouble."

"You better take care of yourself when no girl will even take care of you, when no girl will even look at you," the sister insisted.

"I do not care if they do not look at me," the brother always replied.

"As it is, you are no good in your studies and then your ways of avoiding the girls will never ever make you successful in life, I can bet. You are good to look at but that alone will not take you far," the sister advised.

"I love and care for my mother and she cares for me and that is more than enough for me," suggested Prabhat.

"My dear brother, you are sadly mistaken. Merely having a good face that is attractive will not help you much. It will not carry you far. You need to have attractive manners to entice girls. Then you need to have a good career, and some good position in society. You possess none of these," Jyoti advised.

"Life is a maths equation. In order to gain the most, you have to know how to convert negatives into positive. So, my dear sister, you do not have to worry about me. But, my dear sister, you possess all but better be careful before you are raped and thrown off," the brother retorted

"Shut up bhaiya," the sister replied in anger.

"I am sending a careful note for you, my dear little sister," said Prabhat

"My father loves me," said Jyoti.

"I do not deny that, but that should not get you out of your senses. I am sounding, only sounding a careful signal before you fall down badly looking at the present times and present society," reminded Prabhat.

"I thank you bhaiya. But I am giving you a warning to change your ways, lest you are left alone with your views," spoke Ritu.

"I am ringing a loud bell for you to tell you that all that glitters is not gold and before you fall into a pit, retrace your steps towards safety and decency," the brother advised his sister.

This is how the two quarrelled when they sat together.

On a day, it had gone dark as it was a wintry day. While returning from the market, where his mother had sent him, he found a car standing and heard the cries of a girl. So, he stopped his car and went to see what was going on. What surprised him were two young men tightly holding a girl who was crying, begging to be left. Prabhat came forward and asked them to leave her. They refused and told him to come and join them in enjoyment. He came forward and gave such severe hits that they left her. He asked her to go and sit in his car. After that, he had a ferocious fight with those villains, threw them all and drove the car fast. He asked the girl her address and turned the car in that direction. Geetanjali was still scared wondering if he also had some bad intentions, but he safely reached her to her place. In tears, she requested him to come in and meet her father. But he refused telling her that he would come some other day. Next day, he got her car repaired and came to give it back. Geeta was not at home. So, he introduced himself to her father. "By the way, Geeta has gone out with her mother, but please do sit down and have a cup of tea with me."

Prabhat sat down and he asked him about his father. On knowing his father's name, he said "Oh I know him very well. By the way, what are you doing at the moment?" he asked.

"I am on the way to find a good job," said Prabhat

"I know someone who can help you," said the man who had asked him to sit down.

He took out his letter-head pad and wrote a request letter to his friend to give a good post to this boy. He was none but Geeta's father.

Accordingly, on the request of Geeta's father, Prabhat got a good and a high post in a company where he saw a number of girls also working. Geeta, her name was long, Geetanjali, so people called her usually Geeta. She was also working here. Silently, he started his work and the boss was happy with him. Among the corporate hubs dress is given great importance. All were well dressed sprinkled with scent to show that they had taken their bath and were coming fresh out of their bath tub to start their work. Those that bowed down to their boss despite not good in their work got early promotions. They were often seen sitting together in clubs or gardens. The girls were placed even above those boys that were really good in their work and deserved promotions. These boys were serious and said in many ways that they would not bow down to the wishes of the boss. At times, they felt very hurt. Despite all this, they would continue unless they found some other job and at other times, would leave immediately. Such was the culture of big companies.

In this matter, Geeta was very strict and no one dares even touch her and she was very efficient in her work. Prabhat admired her from a distance. Same could be said about Prabhat, a very handsome, upright fellow, who showed no interest in girls, though many tried to have his attention but failed.

Prabhat was satisfied with his work, but when he was placed under a girl least deserving that post, he left the job and got into another company, though here he missed the company of Geeta. He was happy working here. The work that was given to him was very satisfying and the boss was very much satisfied with his work that he did efficiently.

Prabhat was happy with the work that was given to him and did it with honesty. The boss was very much satisfied with him. Prabhat, after some time was called by the boss, who said, "Here is some work that is not in your nature, but you have to do it as it is the order from above."

"What is it sir?" he asked.

"You have to go for an inspection and pass a hospital that has nothing in it, but they are offering a huge amount for passing it as a good place for training doctors. We shall share some money with you also." "No sir, I do not want such money." He went to see the hospital. He was stunned to see a hospital where the beds for the patients were filled by the beggars of the vicinity. He went and saw to his surprise, no doctors, but men moving about with stethoscope, the use of which they did not know. There were no equipments needed for the hospital. But, to his disgust, papers, had to be filled to say that it was a very good hospital that needed immediate government's recognition. And for this false statement, were five crores offered. Prabhat's hand shook as he filled and signed the papers. Students coming out of such an institute will be killing the patients, though I am sure they will get in few doctors to teach and some equipment later on. Prabhat gave the entire money and refused to share any. When they asked him to do for the second time, he immediately resigned. With his experience, he could now get a job in AIMS. His Geeta was not there. But they met when their duties were over. Seen around there would be groups of four or five boys and girls out to find pleasure. While sitting in the restaurants, they did not mind taking a pinch of wine that would add to their pleasure as they embraced each other.

Education had greatly improved, but all wanted quick results. If you looked around inventions and strange inventions, which the former would have never thought of, came to the fore. Telephone, mobile, C.C.T.V. cameras, T.V., aeroplanes, with more facilities and at cheap rates, were to be seen all around. Picture halls became popular. Though there was improvement all around and it looked as if men had transformed society, there was a severe fall in moral values. Morality lost its meaning. In the dictionary of the times, pleasures at the cost of anything became the central theme. 'Let us enjoy in whatever way we can', became an important issue. Togetherness of opposite sex offered the maximum pleasure. Dresses the girls wore were unique. They wore dresses that maximum showed their body which attracted the opposite sex. In fact, sex became the all-resounding word. Let us enjoy life to the maximum because this valuable time, if gone will not come again. So, make the best of every moment. This beautiful expensive time comes only once in life. So, enjoy it at any and every cost. Can you buy time once it is gone? No. So, let it not pass off. Anything that adds to the pleasure must not be avoided. So, one should not mind using such things as wine, drugs, etc. To entice girls, men would show how rich they were and they would afford the best time for her. At other times, they would scare them with dire consequences if they did not bow down before them to their thirst. The moral standard was further reduced by the impact of the movies. Divorce, dowry deaths and extra-marital relationship became the common features of the times. Wife for home and extra-marital relationship outside became the most common feature of the day.

Real spiritualism was thrown to the winds and a new form of spiritualism was flourishing in the society. Fake gurus came forward to sing, dance and give lectures, but behind all this was the desire to entrap the girls and rape them. Getting dedicated to the gurus and sannyasis who professed to them a spiritual world resulted in molestation and rape. It was then too late to withdraw. They cheated them. Gurus like Asa Ram and Honey were common. It was not possible to withdraw when the girls realised that their world of spiritualism was nothing else, but a business of satisfaction of the sexual desires of the gurus. It was too late for them to withdraw and they were caught into a dirty world. Spiritualism no longer remained a sacred world, but a business where the so-called gurus satisfied their lust and hunger for sex. Rapes increased and became an important feature of the day. Dowry deaths increased as the emphasis was on receiving pleasures, good or bad, that they desired. The need of sex was important in whatever way the men behaved. They were worse than animals by raping their very daughter to whom they had given birth. They would go to the extent of raping a one-year-old child who was innocent and was not aware of what sex meant. What more can be said about men! Spiritualism no longer remained a lesson to follow, but a sort of business, giving men great satisfaction and pleasure. Honey trail gave them satisfaction and a central cause of the so-called show of spiritualism. A back-door entry of many young and innocent girls was all they understood by spiritualism. The love of the Almighty was just a means to entrap young girls who no longer could go out of their dirty circle once they were caught.

The spirit of religion no longer remained a way of feeling of oneness and harmony with all. The greater the identity you feel with others, the more you are religious. What we have seen are the outer garments. Mine and thine destroy the very spirit of true religion.

Kiran needed the healing of her heart, a heart full of love for her father, yet she had betrayed him. He was one of those who imparted the best of education to her. He went out of the way and sent her to study with the boys which was not the culture of the day in her family. He was the happiest when the results were announced and she came out with flying colours. She made him happy as he made her happy. She shared from her heart her very life. Her story was such that it would heal people's heart. She sacrificed her happiness for the good of her sisters. But the parents never understood her. She betrayed her parents, those who had given her so much love and care. Was it the mind? Was it the changing times? What was it by which she betrayed the reputation of her father and the name of the family? She eloped, never cared how the father would feel and what would happen to the younger sisters. Giving out a false excuse, she eloped with Puneet. The father died on hearing this news of a severe heart attack that very night. The father wrote a note saying, "Today I have lost my heart, something I needed to live on. How I will go on I do not know myself, I will try to understand. I know well how badly I have hurt my daughter." On hearing this, Kiran broke into tears and would have rushed to ask for forgiveness, but not now as he was no longer living, so she felt very strongly that she must commit suicide to give her father a proper answer. She started to make herself hang on the fan when by chance Puneet entered her room. He was amazed to see her at what she was attempting.

"What are you up to Kiran? Times have changed and I do not know why your father took it to heart."

"We somehow belong to the old age, trying hard to swallow what is happening today," replied Kiran.

"By giving your life are you helping anyone? Think of your children and then think of me. Do they hold no meaning for you?" asked Puneet

"I am helping myself, Puneet," Kiran spoke softly.

"I really do not see how by destroying your family you are helping yourself. Try to do something that would make your father proud of you and we are all here to help you achieve your goal. The past is over. An inch of time is an inch of gold. But you cannot buy an inch of time with an inch of gold. The time is gone and to repay your father, you should show that you are still his daughter. Do not lose your heart. In such moments, we need to be brave to correct the time that is going its way. Healing does not mean finding and treating every inner scar which sends its message to haunt us. It means going even deeper where we find the light and warmth of our own core qualities of love and peace. They are eternally present within us and they are what we need to heal our wounds. Navratri is approaching, invoke your mother Goddess to whom you are devoted, recognise the need to remove your ignorance with the help of Shakti.

At the mention of Shakti, tears started coming out from the eyes of Kiran and flowing out on her cheeks. Puneet softly wiped her cheeks. She smiled while Puneet lovingly embraced her and said, "Now be brave. With the changing times, we do not know what we have to face. Together we shall have more energy to face. Live your life from your heart. Share from your heart and your heart and your story will heal and touch people's soul. All healing is first the healing of the heart. Come on Kiran, you have to guide your children and live for me without which all will be shattered. Be brave and be kind and all this comes from your heart."

India is facing a big challenge. It is the lack of education that has kept India a nation first slave to the Muslims, then to the Britishers and then to Gandhis. Uneducated, we do not know our rights and gladly we have served as slaves. It well suits the rulers to keep us slaves and rule over us and enjoy the position gained. Education for all is something that is the need of the hour. We need compulsory education till the tenth, so that all well understand their rights and duties, as well, understand their position in the society and in the world. We have struggled for ages and all that we have gained from the government are few buildings where nothing is given in the name of education. This keeps the nation uninformed that voters are the rulers and not the slaves. A bottle of wine is enough to choose their rulers. Centuries have passed, but the fate of the common man remains the same. Illiterate they were and even today they remain the same. Even Modi Ji forgot this priority. What he needed was to make education compulsory for all till high school with good buildings for the schools and good dedicated teachers to impart knowledge. Illiteracy has remained a curse where men do not understand their position and what they need to know. So many years have passed after independence and we stand where we were.

Next is the issue of health. They say health is wealth. A healthy nation takes big stride towards great work being done towards the improvement of the nation. We urgently need good hospitals with hard-working trained doctors free within the reach of all. With these improvements, employment will come to a great extent. Happy, healthy and educated men can make a nation great.

It was the dawn of a new era that was quietly stepping in. What looked prominent was the fall in moral values. Honesty lost its high position and dishonesty was to be seen almost in every field and every corner, in hospitals, in politics, in schools, in business, in trade, in hotels, in the neighbourhood and in technology, with young girls and even in the field of spiritualism. All round the shape of society changed and there ushered in a completely new era. It had its advantages and disadvantages.

What looked prominent was the importance of money. Money became the God even in such a holy field as that of patriotism. There is no such thing as honesty and devotion to the cause of the poor and the country. They lose their sense, the purpose for which they joined this group. Giving long lectures outside about their importance for which they had come up, they forgot the purpose for which they had come in and started making money for their sons and for their own-selves. Getting a large amount of money to be used for the good of the poor, only a little went to the right place. The rest was diverted to their own accounts. Only one village was allotted to one person to look after its welfare, but by the end of the term of five years, the villagers told that they had not seen his face even once! They are considered as dedicated to the good of the nation, but the reality is different. In all different fields as we take a look, we have nothing but despair and disappointment. In some of the hospitals of high repute, a doctor of name and fame told the patient that three valves had to be replaced but the patient on taking a second opinion, he was told that only one had to be taken out and when the operation was performed by replacing one, the patient was all right. The prime minister came with a slogan to end all corruption, has ended with the corruption, even at the level of C.B.I. The police are worse where you can get the most difficult work done by offering bribe. A practising young unmarried doctor was told by her cousin to put the property and money that she was having in his name and account so that he would have it after her death. The doctor refused to do it. So, that very night, she was murdered. The police closed the case saying no clues were to be found, as they were heavily bribed. You are entitled admission in the best institution by behind-the-back practice. "Bharat se bhago" is seen when Malya, Choksi, and Neerav Modi prefer to walk out of India, looting the banks. It is to be seen when the poor die during demonetisation standing in the line while the rich sitting at home got the money. In the name of ending corruption, it has reached to its highest level in all fields of life. Money became their god to be worshipped. Your position in society depended on the amount of money you possessed. Money and mansions are the only wealth. Character, good conduct, wisdom, happiness and enjoyment all depended on how much money you possessed. What looked prominent at the dawn of the era is a fall in the moral values. Girls moved freely with boys. The dress they put would have put us to shame. But now times demanded short skirts, sleeveless blouses all arranged in such a way as to show off the body and made to look sexy which would be their greatest achievement. Sex becomes the buzz-word and more you looked sexy, greater was your achievement. If the boys ran after you, you ought to be proud of yourself. Enjoyment among girls and boys was the goal that young ones ran after. If any comment was made against them, they cared the least. They were cool and felt if one life was given to them, they need not waste it. Why should they bother about the oldies and not live the life as they want it. They do not care to go about as the oldies wished them to go. Why should the old bother about something that did not concern them. The parents were old-fashioned in all their ways of life and they need not interfere in the ways of the young and if they did, the young would prefer to walk out. They were not willing to hear any sex lectures from them. What if *dadi* would have come out of her grave and saw this dance of nakedness!!

Rape became a common feature of the time. Once while Geeta and her colleague were going back to their places and it had gone a little dark, they were stopped by a group of boys who dragged them out of the car and wanted to rape them. Together they fought with courage but how long could they continue to stand against them? Prabhat luckily happened to pass that side, stopped his car and gave a befitting reply to the rogues who ran away. But the girls never saw the difference between the director who kept on sitting in the car not spoiling the crease of his scented coat and never even venturing to look outside fearing that he be dragged out by the hooligans to receive a good beating and on the other side, the young odd and simple-looking boy who stopped to save their respect and honour.

But a good part was that India was emerging with inventions. In many ways, they landed on new technology and new discoveries and new inventions. It gave India a position of pride and fame and a place in the world. They could find that man could survive in other planets like Moon and Mars. Not satisfied, they kept on running to find more in the air, in the sky and on the land. Small families were the fashion of the day. No longer a couple had three or four children. One or maximum two was the fashion of the day. So, they doted upon them. The life of the parents was confined to these children with the result that they grew up as conceited and self-centred. The young were in a hurry to finish their studies and moved fast towards what they wanted to be. They were not willing to sit long and hear what their parents wanted them to be. The lectures bored them and they would rush towards what they wanted to be, it may be right or wrong. They did not need the advice of their parents and their wishes. Oh! no long lectures, on what Krishna said to Arjun or what Tulsi Das said should be the right character of a young man by giving an idealistic character of a person like Ram—all these were very boring and need to be left for the oldies only. For the young, it is the new technology and new discoveries that were important, out of which, still new things could be discovered. An easy life, self confident, conceited, on way to make the most of what they possessed, there was a rush by the young in all possible directions. They wished to make the maximum of what minimum they possessed. In this, they would move on the path that was convenient to them. They belonged to a clique as these were the days of specialisation.

As far as education went, Jyoti was very good. She occupied a high post in the company. She worked hard to understand new technology and how it could be made for the good of the people at large. So far so good, but she must have fun and amusement in the company of the boys of her age. She would dance in which she was an expert. She would sing. She would enjoy drinks with them and did not mind to add some drugs in the drinks. Jyoti was very popular with them and there were many that sought her company. She would often come home very late.

On a day while she was sitting with Prabhat, he cautioned her, "My dear sister, do not come so late because rogues are there out on the streets to catch young girls and rape them."

Jyoti replied, "Bhaiya, why are you so jealous of me? So many are running after me and you do not have a single girl who would seek the company of such a boring teacher."

Prabhat said, “My dear sister, it is no joke and I am warning you of worse consequences. I do not at all trust the boys whose company you keep, specially that boy Ravinder, if I correctly remember his name. They are making a fool of you to take advantage of you.” Prabhat thus cautioned his sister.

His sister Jyoti replied rudely, “Papa and mama do not say anything. Who are you to talk like this?”

“I am your elder brother. Mummy and Papa do not know these boys. What family they are coming from, they do not know, they are rogues as I understand,” advised Prabhat.

“Bhaiya, you better not speak like this about my friends. You need to take care of yourself,” said Jyoti.

“My dear sister, wake up from your slumber for you are living in a fool’s paradise,” reminded Prabhat.

“Thank you Bhaiya,” said Jyoti sarcastically.

“You are living in a fool’s paradise,” reiterated Prabhat.

“Thank you for warning me,” replied Jyoti. “I am going out with my friend on a trip to

Washington for five days and Papa had given me the permission," said Jyoti.

Prabhat insisted that she should not be allowed to go out for a such long period with an unknown person, but the father did not listen to him and his love for the daughter allowed her to go and come back soon. Jyoti was living under a delusion as the age was such that opened the gate of lust and greed.

"Jyoti, you know well that I cannot live without you. So, in no case, you may extend your visit," said the father.

"Oh, no, *Papa* it is the same here. I may be back even earlier." Jyoti spoke emotionally with tears in her eyes. Jyoti bade farewell to *Papa* and *Ma* and went off. She refused to even give a look to her *bhaiya* and moved off.

Money was invented to enable us to share goods and services but it posed major problems. There came a big divide between the rich and the poor. From being created as a means to fulfil the needs, money became to be flaunted as a status symbol. Money because of its purchasing power became a commodity much sought after. Its need amongst some gave rise to theft and corruption.

It was to get money that this fellow deceived the parents and the girl.

Jyoti flew to Washington and was dazed to see so much light that darkness had no place in any corner of the city. The roads were broad and vehicles strictly followed rules. All round there was so much of cleanliness that she felt highly impressed. The friend took her to the market and bought few expensive dresses. She said to him, "Oh! How much you love me?" to which he replied, "More than my life, dear." "Let us go home," said Jyoti. "Let us have some more fun before I take you home. We will go to a restaurant where you will show your talent by making your dance the best ever before. You know all will see your beautiful dance and then we will have some drinks. Thereafter I will take you home."

She had no reason to disbelieve one who had lately led her to understand that if anyone really loved her, it was no one else but this fellow. Cleverly like the modern guys, he had heaped praises on her and told her humbly that he stands no comparison to her talents and beauty. Forgetting herself and always addressing him as darling, and dear she had forgotten to ask even his name. Your actions are your only true belongings. You cannot escape the consequences of your actions. Your actions are the ground on which you stand. Jyoti was no exception to this fundamental rule. One can give the example of a silkworm. She was exactly like it that made the thread of her own substance and spin the cocoon and will, in the course of time, get imprisoned inside. Jyoti had high dreams like the modern girls of today to get into a high rich life of modern times. But it is not about how to receive your dreams, it is about how you lead your life. If you lead your life in the right way, the *karma* will take care of itself. The dreams will come to you.

Jyoti, according to her friend's request, was at her best as her legs quivered with the start of the orchestra and with a forced smile on her face, she moved about. All were enchanted and wanted to touch her, but she with lovely movements went fast from one direction to another. She could see her lover as she looked around. The dance ended and she looked for her lover and found that he was nowhere there. She went to the owner to enquire about him and was told in clear words that she has been sold to him and that he has taken the money and gone off.

She trembled as she heard these words. She enquired about her belongings which she was told he has left in the back room, which she was allowed to collect and move in a room in a nearby hotel. Jyoti trembled to see her future. She had committed a deadly crime of not listening to her brother. She tried to be somebody and remained next to nobody. She has earned her own fate for which she cannot blame anyone. And now she has to undergo a future that she dreaded. She must suffer as there was no way out. She has sown seeds by her own hands, the result of which she has now to undergo. She realised that she has committed a deadly crime the consequences of which glared at her. The passport was taken away from her; she was not been aware of a single person here. She saw her life to dance every evening and spent the night with a new person everyday. She trembled with horror to see what stood before her, and her future she dreaded. Why the father could not stop her as he was an intelligent officer who ought to have known the world and its ways better than anyone, why the mother was silent as if she had no love for me, only the brother was against me but his warning I did not take seriously as he was always against me in my ways of life. Now I must suffer the consequences. The past is over and to brood upon it is a sheer wastage of time. I must think of some method to get rid of this place. She must get off from the clutches of the restaurant owner. The appearance of a new man everyday to take advantage of her beauty and body made her shiver with shame and disgust. On the weekend came at night a very old man. He approached her with shaking head and hands over which he had no control. She hated to see such a man. She gave a heavy push to this man who fell down and fainted. She was sure he would not recover till morning. She put her clothes out of the box into a bag and smartly walked out. On the enquiry by the gate man, she told him the she was going to get some eatables in the bag as the royal was hungry. The gate man had no reason to disbelieve her and out of the sight of the gate man, she started running fast. Where? She herself did not know but only out of the reach of that gateman and restaurant owner. She ran always looking back to make sure that no one was following her. It was at this time that she stuck against an old lady who fell down. She quickly put her up and said, "Sorry *Ma*," when she realised that she had hurt an old Indian woman. The word "*Ma*" made her look at her closely and she said, "Where are you running away, my child in the darkness of this night. You can come and stay with me at night and start your race in the morning." She happily accepted her suggestion.

A place to hide her head in a familiar surrounding was all that she needed the most at this moment and this was the safest place. They earned money from their different jobs, put it together and lived a happy life. They earned more than what they could earn in India and lived with a good standard. They were old, not looked after well by their sons and daughters-in-law. They suggested Ritu to join them. "But what is your problem that at this tender age you were running away in the darkness of a winter night?" asked one of them. Ritu was quiet for some time, but another one fearing some trouble might not come as she was young and beautiful, said "Have you been turned out by your husband." The third wanted to know if she has left the house because the husband had her to get out and get some more money from her parents. Poor Ritu, the name now changed to hide her identity was dazed at the queries and was silent. In after-thought, she said, "I want a job at a safe place and live happily earning for myself." All were satisfied as her aim was the same as theirs. "We will help you as your aim is similar to ours. You are scared to go out so we will find such a job. In the meantime, you would do the household jobs here in the house when we are out."

Jyoti was quiet, but readily agreed as she was learning to grow from inside out. She was happy doing all types of jobs, but when it came to washing dishes, tears would roll out of her eyes as if life meant only this for her. But it did not take long for them to find a job of looking after a small child of one-year-old whose mother had died during the delivery. The father was a young high-ranking police officer. He interviewed a number of girls and grown-ups, but found Ritu as the best. In her appearance she was far too good, neat, good looking and speaking good English fluently. While going to his office, he would leave the child with Ritu and on coming back, would take him away.

In no time the child got fond of Ritu whom he addressed her as *Didi*. Ritu was given a handsome amount for her work. She gave all the money to the elderly ladies with whom she was living. Her heart wept to go back home, but had no means, so she was staying. She never asked for the extra she was contributing and never felt that she was better than others. Humbly, she lived without any arrogance. In fact, she felt obliged that she was saved from a dirty life that was forced upon her. At times, she cursed herself for not listening to her brother. She felt that her Bhaiya was outdated and her pride consisted in so many boys running after her. But now that very pride had thrown her into a pit of disaster. Whenever she was alone, she cried bitterly.

Time passed and the child became too fond of her company and when the father would come to take him back, he was not willing to go with him and asked *papa* to take *didi* also with him. Each and every day the father promised to take her with him the next day before he would leave his *didi*.

Here in India when she did not return for ten days, the father became nervous. The mother was sad and saw what the son predicted. The father asked Prabhat to do something. "What can I do? I told you not to let her go for more than a day, but you were mad after her willing to let her do what she wanted. I warned you *papa* but what can I do now. *Papa* you have not even noted his name. You saw him well dressed with fine and expensive dress on and you allowed her to go. Being aged and having more intelligence, you got yourself to be cheated by a fool. I kept on warning you, but you always feel that your daughter is very intelligent and your son is a fool. You silenced me. You have always silenced me and made me understand that in intelligence, I stand no comparison to your daughter. And now you are asking me to go and find her out. It is such a big city. Without any address, it will be absolutely useless to go there.

The son was right but the father was almost mad and did not see the folly that he had committed in his too much love for his daughter. He cried like a child and begged Prabhat to help him out. The age was like this. A smart fellow, good in appearance and with great show was respected while an honest fellow with a simple dress was considered a fool.

A father who considered his son a fool was now his only hope, someone he felt would do any useful work for him. The memory of the daughter made him to lose his appetite and he refused to take food. The wife told him that he was doting upon her so much that she was a spoiled child and thought of herself so much that her feet were not on the ground. "So many times I warned you, but you would not listen to me, the consequences of which you have to bear," said Kiran. "In our times, even in the neighbourhood, we were not allowed to go without permission. You gave her the liberty to go anywhere with anyone she wanted, the result of which you see now. I do not see any point in killing yourself. She is clever enough to come back at any time she wants. So, stop punishing yourself because we all need you so much. Prabhat is a simple boy who would surely do his very best to trace her out. He very much loves his sister and, that is why, he was quarrelling with her when he did not agree with her ways." Kiran also suffered being a mother, but was absolutely silent. She could see that it was entirely the mistake of her husband, so she was quiet about it. She had seen how continually he was insulting the son as he did not look smart like his daughter.

The times believed in outward show. You may be a rogue, but if you dressed up smartly in expensive clothes, spoke English smartly and had manners that attracted others, the society passed you as one most needed. While one who was on the road at night to find a prey to rape and have fun, the other fellow simple, unattractive would step down to save the honour of the girl. While one with pride moved about getting attention from all around, the other would be satisfied in doing his work humbly and with honesty, never ever bothering about his looks or any other thing he possessed.

It was an age of show, but it was also an age of new discoveries and new inventions in all fields of life. Prabhat possessed an active mind that worked in this direction. But, he never made a show of it. He had once saved Geetanjali, ever since then both had some feelings for each other. They were working in the same company and often in their free hours, would sit down and talk to each other. Soon they became fond of each other, but never behaved in the manner the times demanded. Prabhat never came forward to hold Geetanjali's hand. They sat and talked, but never went forward in the way times demanded from the young lovers, but the expression of their eyes did tell them that they liked each other. Prabhat would often talk about Geetanjali when he sat with his mother. He loved his mother and very much respected her. Father always looked down upon him, but he found great consolation in the company of his mother. In fact, it was she who gave him the courage not to fall down as he was not the product of the age and was one who had given up all hopes to rise and compete. It was his mother who held his hand and made him to run.

A new age dawned which brought in new innovations in different fields of life. The era of old methods comes to an end. Communication with the help of telephone and mobiles made life easy and comfortable. You could talk to anyone, at any place and any time. New modes to move about in the sky, in the waters and on the land were coming up to give a new direction to the age. Technology afforded a better life. Innovations made the age to sparkle as never before. A move towards better education and an attempt to educate all, the poor and the unprivileged was a great step that was taken towards making the society move forward to better times. Prabhat would often talk about Geeta when he sat with his mother. He loved his mother and respected her. The father looked down upon him, but the company of his mother was a great consolation to him to show his worth. Here, in India, he found a good scope to expand himself. He was in the section of medicines and was successful in finding a new medicine in treating some liver problem that was taking the lives of many. The disease was considered fatal, but Prabhat found a way out of it. His newly found cure was very effective. He gave a cure that gave to the patients new hope and a new life to them. He received a number of awards from different countries. Encouraged, he worked harder in a new way and found cure for some other diseases related to liver. These diseases that appeared small in the beginning, but later on, assumed dangerous proportions that proved fatal. He was highly praised and was a recipient of many awards in India and abroad. Life in this hospital was free from tensions. Intelligent as he was, he could do his work freely. As his name and fame grew, he took remarkable steps in many directions. In no time, this simple ordinary-looking boy did wonders in taking big strides in all directions in the field of medicines. He was called in by Washington University to deliver a series of lectures and for which he received great rewards. He had hopes that hearing his name, his sister would come to meet him. But his hopes remained hopes and no Jyoti came to meet him. Prabhat tried his level best, but in vain. Had Prabhat been interested in drinking and visiting places to see the dance, he might have seen or known about his sister, but as he was averse to all such things, it was not possible to get any clue. Every time he returned, the father looked at him with hopes but was unhappy as nothing could be gained despite his best efforts. The father considered him as a useless fellow and had little hopes from him. He was simple, not a dashing figure like his Jyoti, neither smart, nor well dressed, only good in his work. His wife had made her son Prabhat like that and the father always disliked him but at the moment, he was his only hope. It is an age of show and so simplicity suffered the most. All that glitters is not gold, but people did not understand this and were running after pomp and show. The age, however, had great value in this pomp and show, however hollow it may be. Geetanjali's father never wanted his daughter to get married to this simple, odd-looking boy and he never wanted her to go along with him, but once he got a high name as a doctor and got fame all over in the society and even in the outside world, he asked his daughter to go and give the family's greetings to his mother. So, on that pretext, she went to his place. The father was now keen on Prabhat getting married to Geetanjali. They met sometimes to say a sweet 'hello' or at other times shook hands and said quietly through their eyes how nice it would be to be together, but beyond that, they never said and did anything. The father was never in favour of marrying his daughter to Prabhat, but now on Prabhat getting name and fame in society, he became keen on his daughter getting married to Prabhat. He asked Geeta to go and congratulate Prabhat's mother on the achievement of her son. He cautioned her to behave in an old-fashioned way if at all she wanted to win the mother's heart. It was very important because for Prabhat, the mother was everything. All this he has gathered from his father. Anything that was unpleasant to the mother would be unacceptable to Prabhat. He almost worshipped his mother. He was all the making of his mother. It was a pleasant winter evening. Prabhat as usual was sitting with his mother when a sharp doorbell rang. Prabhat went to see who it was and was surprised to see Geetanjali there.

"Anything special that you have come at this time to my place?" asked Prabhat.

"I was going this way to the market and your house coming on the way, I thought I might meet you and your mother of whom you talk so much."

"Something special," asked Prabhat.

"You will not open the door and ask me to come in, but keep on asking questions," said Geeta much disgusted.

"Oh, I am really very sorry. Do come in. Mother is free and will be happy to meet you," said Prabhat.

"That will give me an opportunity to see her and also pay my respects to her and give my compliments to her on your achievement," said Geeta.

"So nice of you. Come in. Mother at the moment is free. She will be happy to meet you," said Prabhat.

Geeta came in and touched the feet of Kiran with great respect and said, "*Ma,* I have come to give my compliments to you on the great success of your son."

Kiran asked her to take a chair and sit down, but Geeta preferred to sit on the carpet spread on the ground near Kiran's feet. Kiran was touched by such behaviour as she was reminded of her good old days. The present were the days of a handshake and an equal chair next to the elders. Geetanjali broke the silence, "*Ma,* my compliments to you for the success of your son." Kiran was overwhelmed, smiled softly and said, "Thank you my dear child."

"*Ma*, Geetanjali sings very well." So, Kiran looked at Geetanjali and spoke softly with a smile, "Would you like to sing for me too, my child?" The way the mother spoke was not only loving, but would attract anyone to whom it is addressed. She was quiet for some time thinking hard which song to sing when Prabhat jumped in and told her to sing some rousing love song from a film, "Pyar Kiya to Darna Kya." Geetanjali corrected him and told him that before the gurus we do not sing such songs. She chose to sing a song that was the favourite of Meera Bai. Geetanjali sang so beautifully in her sweet voice, "*Meera ke prabhu girdhar nagar doosro na koi,*" hearing which Kiran was greatly impressed. "Who taught you this song?" "My mother, she is a highly religious lady and has taught me quite a number of such songs. She is a lady dedicated to GOD AND TO THE SERVICE OF MANKIND and spends most of her time in spiritual activities. It is something rare in this age. She was much pleased to hear all this. She felt happy and she spoke in a sweet tone, "On my request you sang and did it so beautifully also. I quite agree with your views that are not so much the views of the present society, though much can be said about it also." She stopped for a moment and then took a chain which she was putting on and put it round the neck of Geetanjali. She was quite perplexed at her behaviour, but Kiran spoke softly with a smile on her face, "My dear child, take it as an *ashirvad* from a mother to her daughter." It left Geeta speechless. Geeta stood up and touched Kiran's feet and said, "I am getting late and mother will be getting worried and so I must leave with your permission." She looked pretty in her light blue saree tucked at places with shining pins. She had long hair with a pin that had a bright rose in it. She was so simple, yet looked so enchanting. She looked more a pretty girl of Kiran's times. She had a fair complexion and was tall in stature. She could stand no comparison to her dashing Ritu but was much to the liking of Kiran and Prabhat. When she went away the only question she asked Prabhat, "You like this girl, Prabhat?" Prabhat was shy and silent. She understood the meaning and said "I too approve of your choice and bless you both."

Poor Ritu was carrying on with her drudgery and was reconciled to her fate and felt that this was the safest place and here she could pass her life as others were passing. So, the life went on when the master would drop his son at Ritu's place. Ritu called the child Baloo. The child was quick to run to his *didi*'s arms. But, at this moment, the situation was taking another turn. It was the father that was slowly moving towards Ritu. He did not need her, but the stability in the heart was shaken. He was slowly but surely moving towards her. He was breaking the bondage of position and nationality. As Morgan touched her hand while handing over the child, a wave of thrill passed over his body of which Ritu was absolutely unaware. While the child would refuse to go with his *papa*, he would get an opportunity to talk to her for a while. True love knows no boundaries and here was a heart that was moving towards one who was unaware of it.

Then came a special great day. It was Baloo's birthday. Friends and relations were invited. But, for Baloo, the most important person was his *didi* who was not brought in. The child refused to cut the cake or even stand up to dance. Morgan finding no way out sent his car to bring in Ritu. She took out from her bag a beautiful dress which her *papa* had given her. She dressed up properly in the best way and soon reached Baloo's place. All present were shocked at her beauty and the way she carried herself. Baloo came running and jumped to see her. "Let us have some dance and her dance went on for some time. She took up Baloo and moved amongst others with her ways that charmed all that were present. She then gave the knife to Baloo and asked him to blow the candle off and cut the cake. She sang in her melodious voice, "Happy birthday dear Baloo" as Baloo with her help cut the cake. There was a heavy clapping. Morgan's eyes were for all the time on one person and that was Ritu. He admired her from all angles as if she has come down from heaven to earth. But Ritu was completely unaware of any such feeling that the master was having. He was gradually but surely being attracted by Ritu, though she was completely unaware of what was going in the mind and the heart of her master. But she well knew the feelings of the little child. Unaware and uninterested, she well played the role of a girl who had come to play the role of an *ayah* to hide herself from the clutches of a villain master.

On Sundays, Morgan planned out picnics for the child primarily to enjoy the company of Ritu. They would sing and dance and Morgan would enjoy Ritu's company. But, Ritu was unaware as to what was going on in the heart of her master. All that she knew was that she had come out to make Baloo happy. Unaware and uninterested, she well played the role of a girl who had come to do this job to hide herself from the clutches of a master who was a villain. Morgan brought packets and things to eat that all enjoyed when on Sunday they planned for a picnic. They spent the day smiling, playing and singing. Morgan was happy that Ritu was by his side and he felt that he was in heaven. Ritu played with the child and made him happy. But she never dreamt that with the child, she was making someone else happy too. The child would laugh, and jump into the arms of his *didi* and give her a kiss. Morgan sat enjoying and felt that there was no better way of passing the day and wished that it was longer. Ritu was happy that the child got time to spend outside the lodge that she lived in.

Come another Sunday, they were out to see a movie meant for the children. Morgan was there with him for he would not miss the opportunity to sit by the side of Ritu, one he loved. At times, he would touch her body and a wave of magic passed through his body. What was happening he did not know and in no time, he would have proposed to her. The other three ladies seemed to understand it but as Ritu was absolutely unaware, they did not talk about it.

There was a nearby park where Ritu in the evening would take Baloo out to run about and often played hide and seek. It so came to pass that Ritu fell sick and, in order that Baloo may not catch the infection, sent words that Baloo should not be sent to her. Immediately, he sent a doctor to look into her illness and asked the cook to take care of Baloo.

The doctor advised that she should be admitted in the hospital. Admitted in a costly hospital under the care of a good doctor, she soon started getting better. Morgan after his office hours would come and sit by her side and talked to her. When she became all right, she came back to her place.

Morgan looked and saw a large river meandering from one country slowly along for miles passing from one country to another without stopping. He also saw a huge forest extending along several borders. To his mind two worlds leaped into one – commonality and interdependence. We are all one. Ritu from India and Morgan from America made no difference. The life started as usual. Ritu and Baloo would come out and had great fun. One day while they were running to catch each other to the disgust of Baloo, a van stopped and a black man got down from a van that stopped abruptly and putting his hand over the mouth of Ritu, put her in the van and carried her away. The child started crying and came inside and told the *ammas* present in the lodge that *didi* had been carried away by a black demon. She was put in the van on which they came and carried her away. When *ammas* told the story to Morgan, he was taken aback. She had never told her dreadful story to anyone. She was ashamed to speak to anyone despite *ammas* enquiring about it.

Morgan kept on thinking. The girl was so special for the child, but more than that, she was so close to his heart. He would not allow the matter just to pass off like that. But how to tackle it was a great puzzle. He himself went to the park and found out that the C.C.T.V. camera could only catch the number of the van. The man who took her off, his back was only visible. From the registration office, he got the name of the owner but when he came he told that his van had been stolen last month and despite his best efforts, he has not been able to find it. Morgan sent police squads to catch the van running in the northern area. The van was stopped on one barricade and two men sitting inside it were brought before Morgan, the police commander heading the entire police section. The child was missing his *didi*, but more than that was Morgan missing one very close to his heart. The case could not be left just as any case where no solution could be found. Morgan ordered these men to be beaten that they come out with some information. They were beaten so badly that they came out with the name of the Restaurant owner for whom they were working.

Morgan in a strange dress and appearance came to the restaurant and gave a good amount of money to the guard as the tip and asked him the name of the owner. He was also told that he would get some more money if he told him that he could get a girl for two nights. Thereon the guard told him that the master was very much in this business and he could easily get a girl. Morgan was introduced to the owner as a very rich guy wanting a girl for two nights. Morgan wanted to see the type of girls that he could provide before he took one. The girls were shown on a large canvass one by one. Morgan was highly disappointed as he could not see his Ritu as they came one by one on the canvass. At the moment, sir, we have a poor lot, but if you can wait for a week, we are expecting a real good lot. Morgan went through the lot slowly and was not happy because so far he could not see one he was searching. When the last one was shown, she came up with the comment from the owner, "Your Excellency would not approve of this girl." She was a shy Indian girl, who was no one else than his Ritu. When Morgan came out, he told his team to ask the customers to lie down on the ground and to shoot in the air and catch all the girls and put them in their custody. There were heavy shots from both the sides. Finally, the owner was defeated and taken into custody of the police. The owner was asked how he got the Indian girl. It was told that an Indian boy sold the girl to him. The boy was summoned who gave her passport and address. He was also beaten and put behind the bars. The brother was called and the sister handed over. She clasped her brother and in tears told him, "Bhaiya, you were right only that I should have listened to you. Morgan has saved me from that dirty life of a dancing girl and one who had to accept a new man every night. Finding no way out, I would have committed suicide. The restaurant owner would have never let me go from his clutches." Morgan took Prabhat to his place and while they were leaving for India, he presented him a golden watch fixed with emeralds. Prabhat was hesitant accepting such a rich gift but, when he insisted saying, "New year is in the offing, this is a small gesture towards understanding that we shall ever be friends always standing for each other in times of ease and difficulties," he readily accepted it.

Ritu and Prabhat left for India giving a long, loving kiss to Baloo and a gesture of thanks to Morgan. The father was overjoyed even to think that he would be meeting his daughter soon, something for which he had given up all hopes. He would not have lived long without her, but the good news of her coming would have equally harmed him. So, the good news of her coming was given to him gradually. Ritu, they say, has been found. The culprit has been caught. She has been released from his clutches. Measures were taken to bring her to India. And, finally, the brother was called to verify and bring her back, so that she may reach home within a week. All this was done on the advice of a doctor who said that even good news told all of a sudden can bring about a heart attack. The life of the father had to be saved. An atmosphere of hope and happiness prevailed when Ritu came to India with her brother. As she landed here, the first thing that she did was to salute her mother land leaving which she had seen so much of misery and humiliation. Next she ran to hold her father and with tears in her eyes could only say, "I missed you so much, *papa*." The father overjoyed could only give her a smile.

Geeta's father never wanted his daughter to get married to this simple and ordinary, looking doctor, Prabhat. But when his name and fame grew, he got interested in him and he was quick enough to send a proposal to his father for him for his daughter. It was readily accepted by his father. A prestigious doctor of name and fame was getting married, so dignitaries from all sections of society were invited. Morgan with Baloo was also cordially invited and they were also present. Soon the marriage bells rang. The Indian ceremonies were followed with songs and dances and merry-making that made everyone to enjoy the various functions. It was something so new and something so enjoyable. Good and delicious food was served. All this was much liked by Morgan and Baloo.

It was at this time that Morgan proposed to Ritu. She was taken aback. A person holding such a high position should ask for an ordinary girl came as a great surprise to Ritu. She readily accepted and one more function was there performed with greater pomp and show. Ritu, now Mrs. Morgan, enjoyed dancing and singing with Morgan. He highly appreciated the Indian ways. He requested Ritu's father to accompany them and be with them for a fortnight for he was remembering his father who had recently passed away. Ritu also wanted to be with his father for some time. This was agreed by all so they all, went to Washington leaving Kiran with Prabhat and Geetanjali. Prabhat will go on his honey-moon trip when the father would return. The father would feel better because he was missing his dear daughter for a pretty long time. To be with her will give him immense satisfaction.

Kiran sat in her garden and strange thoughts came running within her. Her father whom she loved so much gave away his life because she married Puneet, one who was not of her caste. But today a marriage has been celebrated where caste did not matter. She looked at a large tree that seemed to talk to her. It said, "Look at me, I have been here for more than hundred years, watching and breathing. I am a silent spectator of many years as they unfold themselves. A silent witness of how people change as time goes on."

My father who loved me so much gave his life because I married out of caste. Today a marriage has been celebrated out of caste with great pomp and show and with so much of happiness. Yesterday, it was my husband who married me and being of caste that was different from mine my father had a heart attack. Tomorrow you never know that in case of same caste marriage, there may be a heart attack. How time in taking its long stride brings about changes that we never thought of. Things change drastically from one generation to another, we never know. But one thing remains true for all times to come is our interdependence. If you go a little deeper, you realise that life is nothing but a play, and one should not take it seriously. The minute you take it seriously, you are sure to get into trouble. The very attitude of seriousness is the root cause of all anxiety. Take it easy. Take it as fun. Really, life is nothing but a drama, well realised by Shakespeare!

❑❑❑

